For Clarice, Maggi, and Jemma – N.W.

For my father, Georges Balit,
and his Alexandrian school days – C.B.

First published in the United States of America in 2006 by
Walker Publishing Company, Inc.
Distributed to the trade by Holtzbrinck Publishers

First published in the United Kingdom in 2006 by Frances Lincoln, Ltd.

For information about permission to reproduce selections from
this book, write to Permissions, Walker & Company,
104 Fifth Avenue, New York, New York 10011.

Library of Congress Cataloging-in-Publication Data
available upon request

ISBN-10: 0-8027-9561-7
ISBN-13: 978-0-8027-9561-8

Visit Walker & Company's Web site at
www.walkeryoungreaders.com

Printed in Singapore

2 4 6 8 10 9 7 5 3 1

THE SCARAB'S SECRET

Nick Would

Illustrations by
Christina Balit

WALKER & COMPANY

NEW YORK

THE PHARAOH'S PAINTERS have just finished decorating his new temple. I like the stars most of all. Aren't they beautiful?

By special request of the pharaoh, I have been painted, too. There, on the far wall, just below the man with the head of a jackal—that's me, Khepri, the scarab beetle. And this is the tale of how I came to be honored . . .

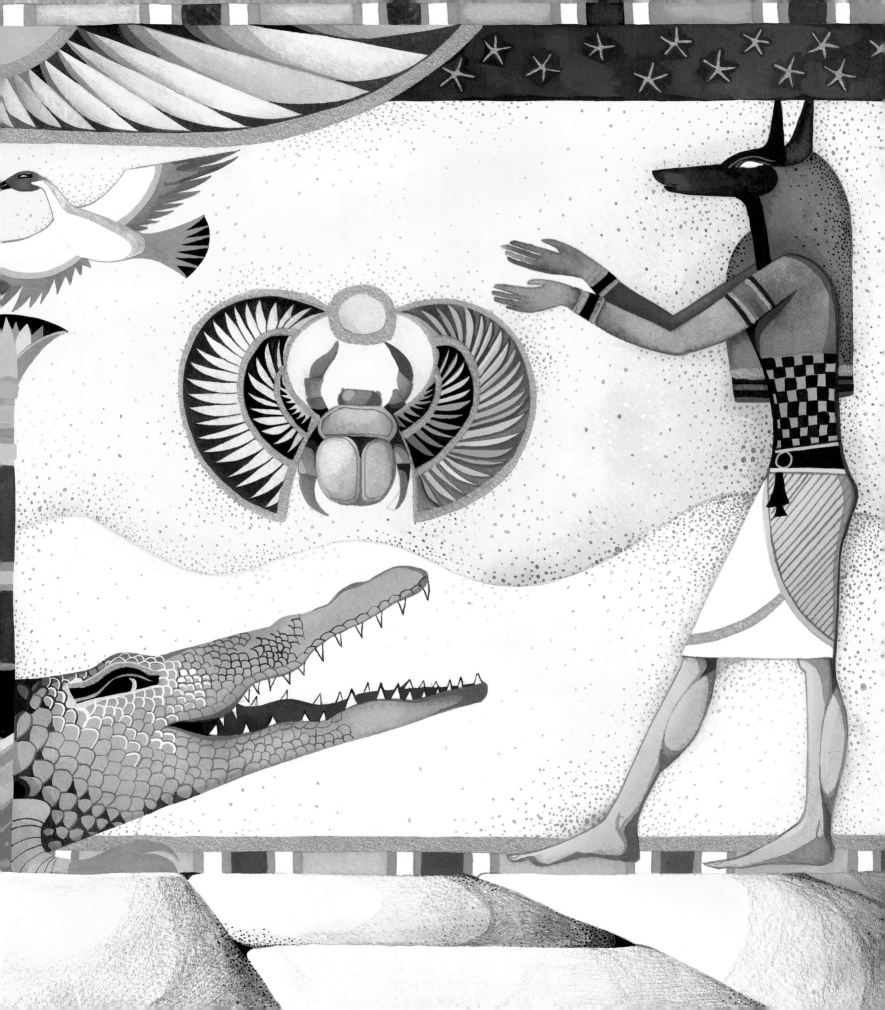

EVERY MORNING, I would set out from the shelter of the temple walls, down to the great river, looking for food and soaking up warmth. When the sun was high, I burrowed among the roots of a tree, under a stone.

But one morning was different. I looked up, and there, in front of the temple, stood a young man dressed in the robes of a prince. He stopped, bent down, and scooped me up in the palm of his hand. I was not afraid. A feeling of peace filled me.

"So," he said softly. "The rising sun shines down on me, and yet I hold the sun in my hand—for, Khepri, your name means 'rising sun.' You are well named and well found."

Then he gently put me back on the ground and whispered, "We shall meet again, you and I."

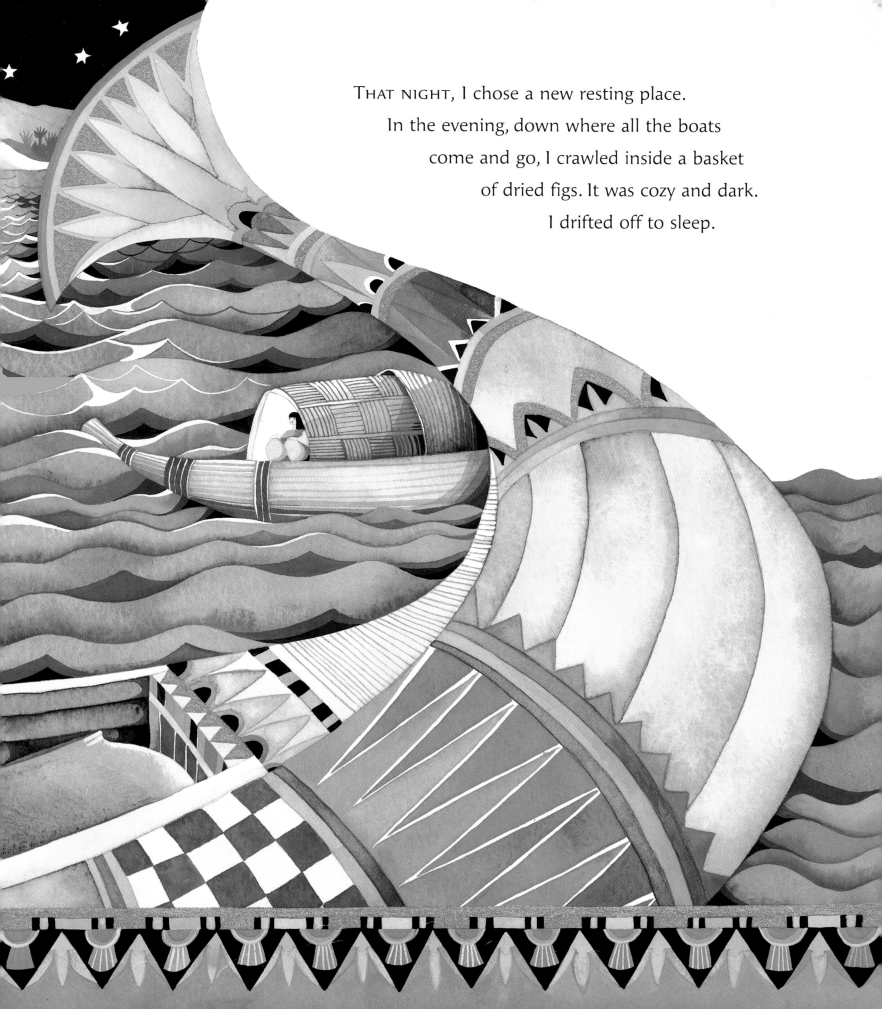

THAT NIGHT, I chose a new resting place.
In the evening, down where all the boats
come and go, I crawled inside a basket
of dried figs. It was cozy and dark.
I drifted off to sleep.

WHEN I WOKE, the basket was swaying, and I heard the chatter of voices. Where was I going? Cold surrounded me. I was being carried down steps.

With a jolt, the basket was dropped onto a hard stone floor. I could hear ringing hammers and chisels. Men were singing.

I crawled out and scurried into the shadow of the wall.

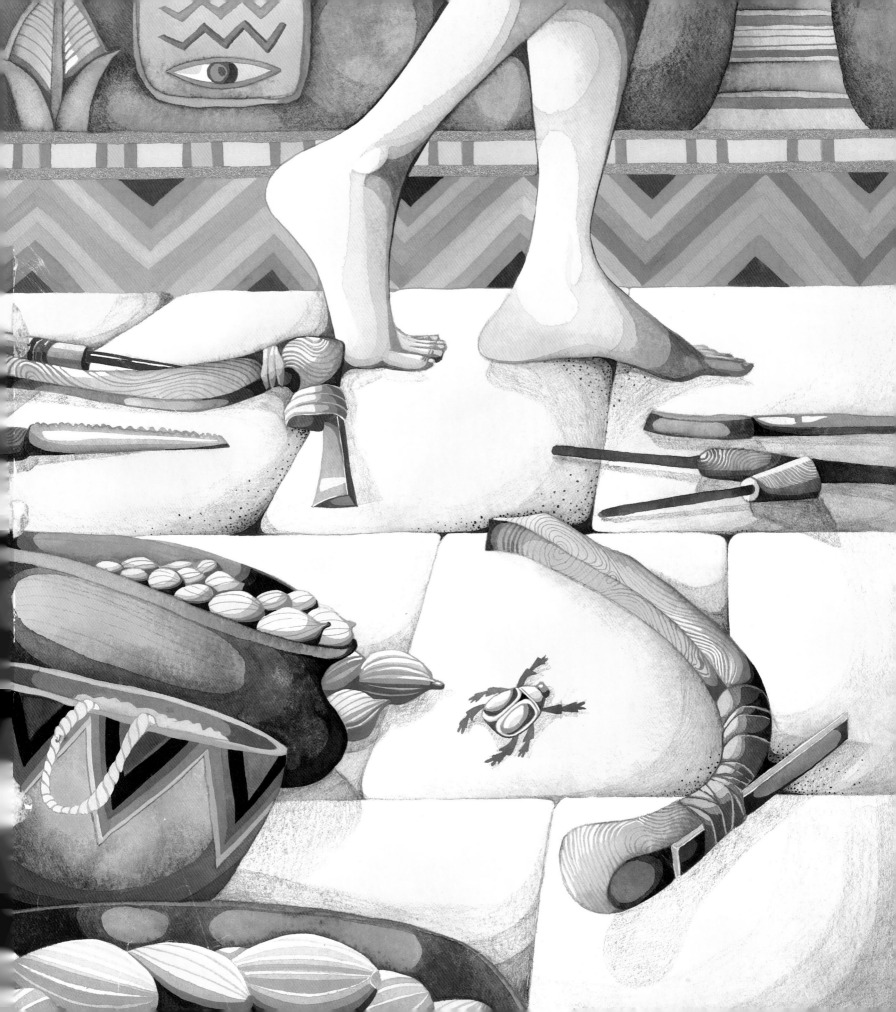

WHEN I TURNED BACK, the basket was gone. The men had all disappeared. I was alone, and I was frightened. Perhaps there was another way out. Keeping to the shadows, I crawled along and soon came to a fork. I took the left passage. The air felt colder. The light from the torches dimmed.

SUDDENLY, I STOPPED. I sensed danger. Very, very slowly I took a step forward—and then I felt it: a crack in the smooth floor, so fine even I could hardly see it. It ran across the hall.

Why was it there? I jumped across it, and as I landed, I knew why. The stone slab beneath me gave way, sank down, and then rose back up. It was perfectly balanced, like a feather on a knife's edge.

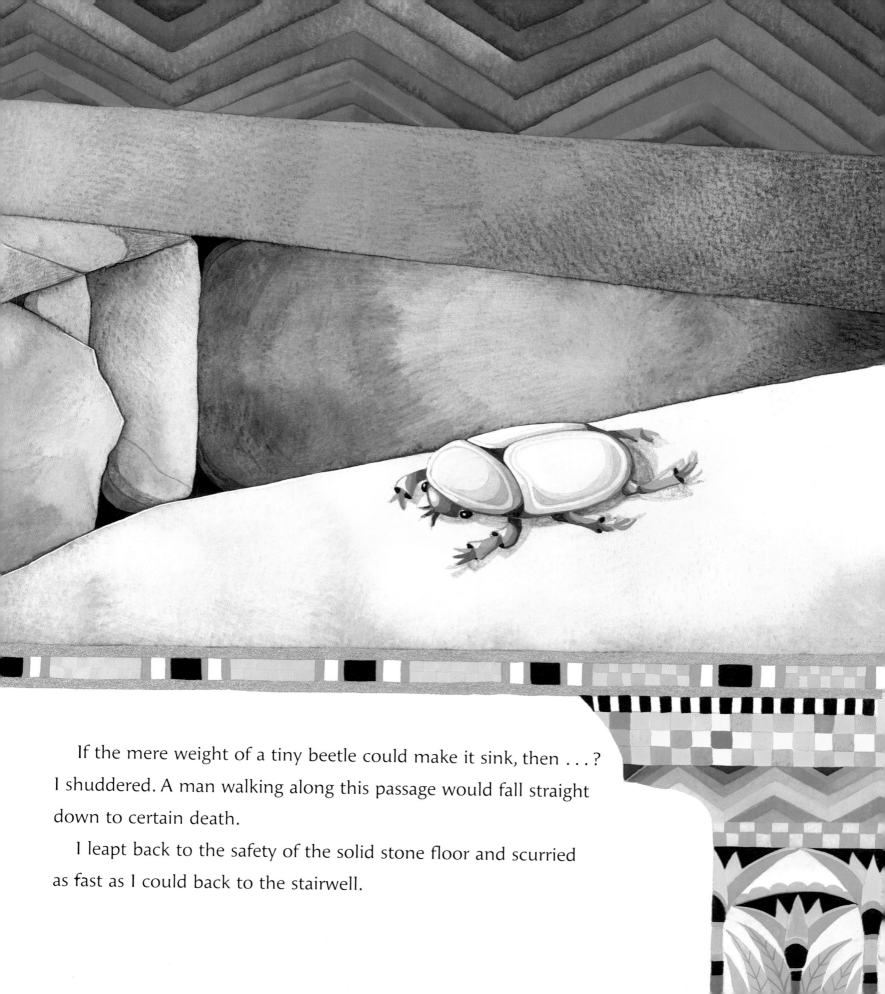

If the mere weight of a tiny beetle could make it sink, then . . . ?
I shuddered. A man walking along this passage would fall straight
down to certain death.

I leapt back to the safety of the solid stone floor and scurried
as fast as I could back to the stairwell.

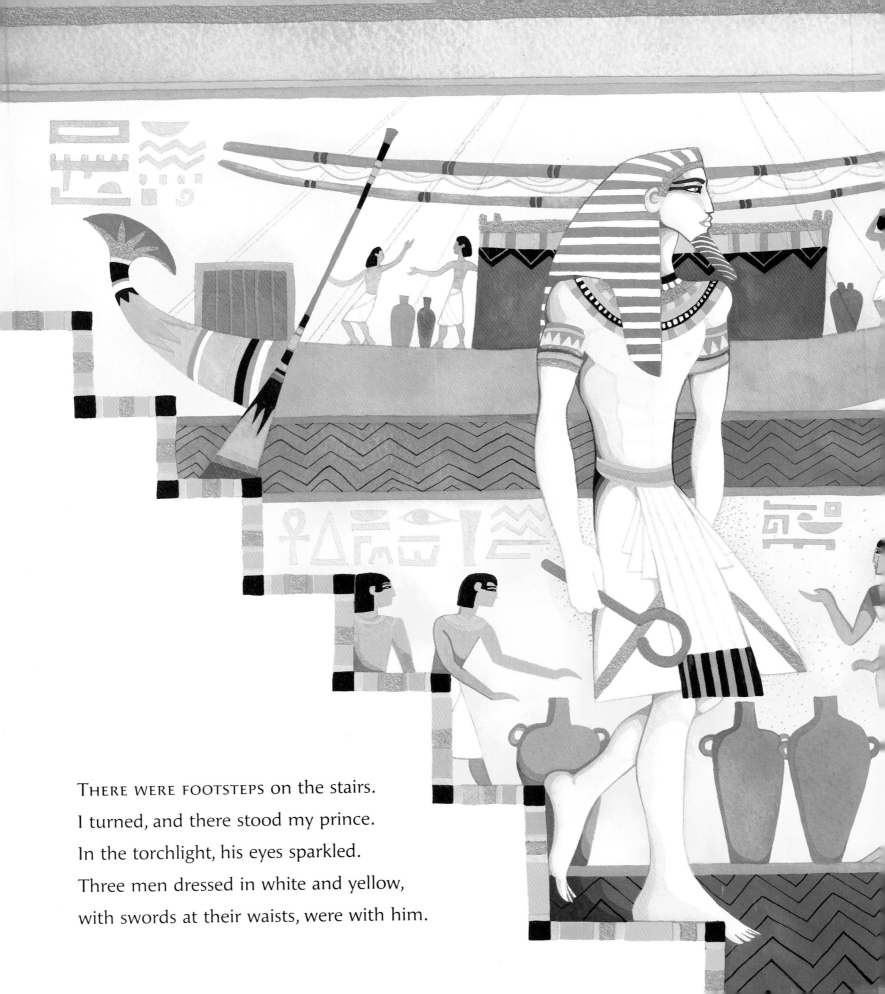

THERE WERE FOOTSTEPS on the stairs.
I turned, and there stood my prince.
In the torchlight, his eyes sparkled.
Three men dressed in white and yellow,
with swords at their waists, were with him.

I HID IN A CORNER as the men went from chamber to chamber. The prince was inspecting the work. While he visited the largest room, I waited in the passage that led to the fork.

The four men approached. "This way, Your Highness," said one, and he pointed down the left fork.

I wished I could cry out, "NO!" If the prince went down there, he would die. Surely the men knew that? And then I realized—of course they knew. That was why the tomb was empty. There were to be no witnesses to the prince's death, apart from a lowly beetle—me.

The prince stopped, eyed each man in turn, and then asked in a clear voice, "Are you sure this is the passage we take?"

"Yes, Your Majesty."

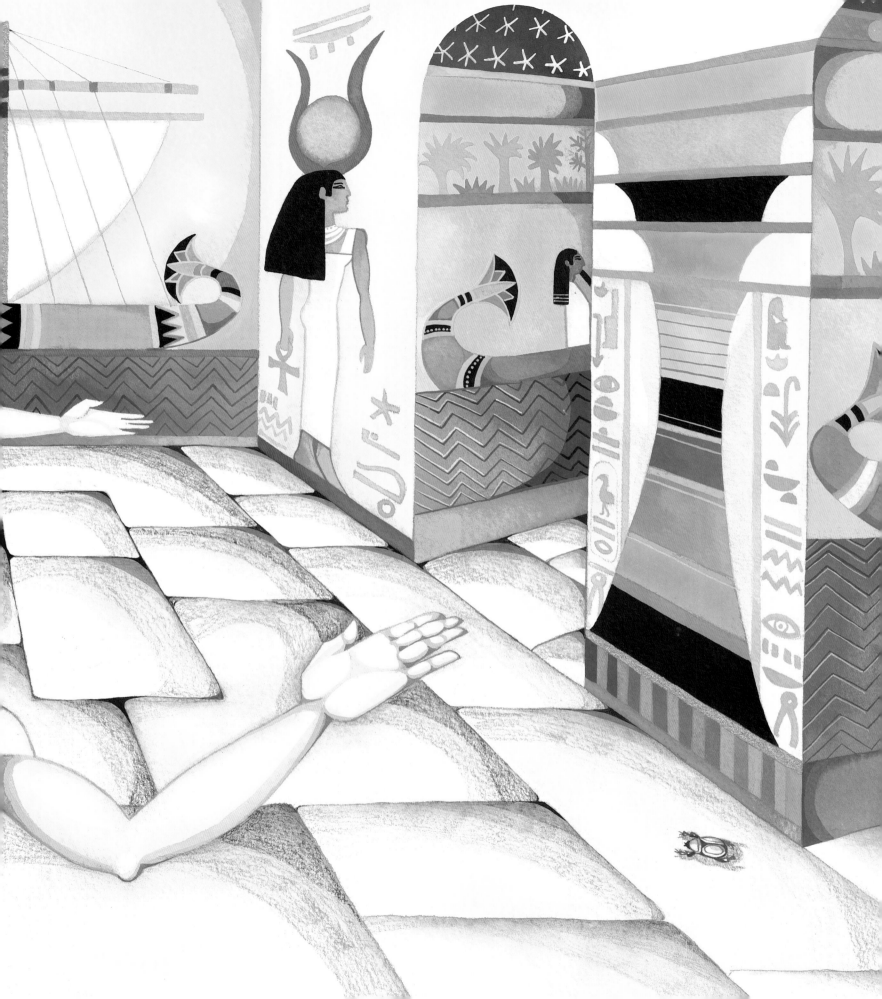

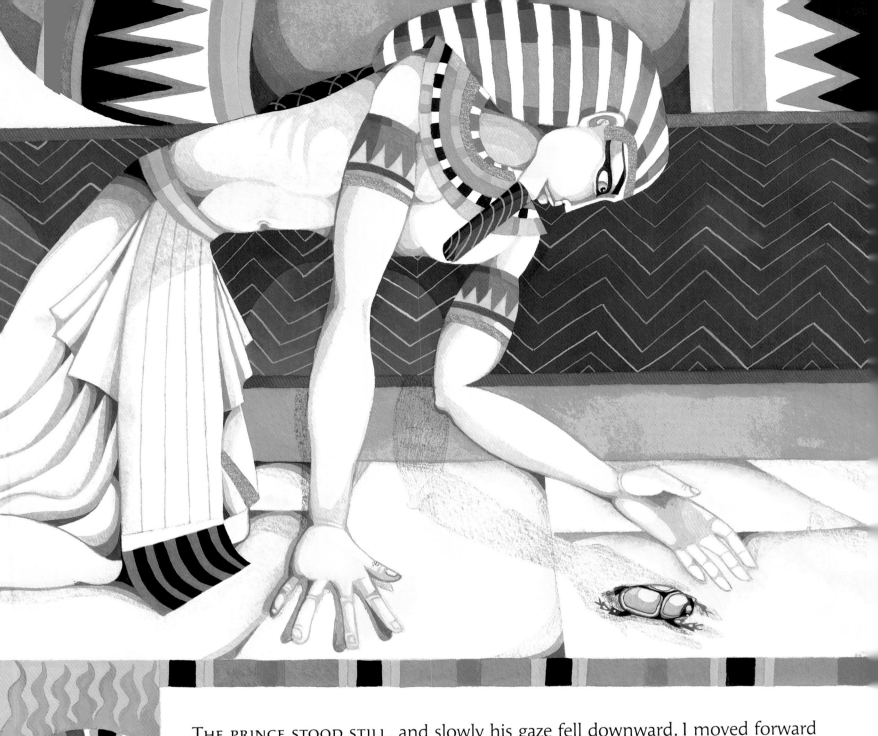

THE PRINCE STOOD STILL, and slowly his gaze fell downward. I moved forward into the light.

A faint smile flickered across his face. "Khepri, we meet again."

The men glanced nervously at each other as he knelt and scooped me up.

"The great god Ra created all things," declared the prince. "This beetle is as precious to Ra as the pharaoh himself. Ra has placed him here for a reason."

"What reason could that be?" asked one of the men anxiously.

"To guide me in my hour of need," replied the prince. "Let us place the beetle at the fork. Whichever way he goes, I will follow."

The prince put me down.

Slowly but surely, I moved toward the passage on the right.

"Look—Khepri has chosen for me, and I shall follow his lead," said the pharaoh. "But before I do, I would like you three to lead me down the other passage."

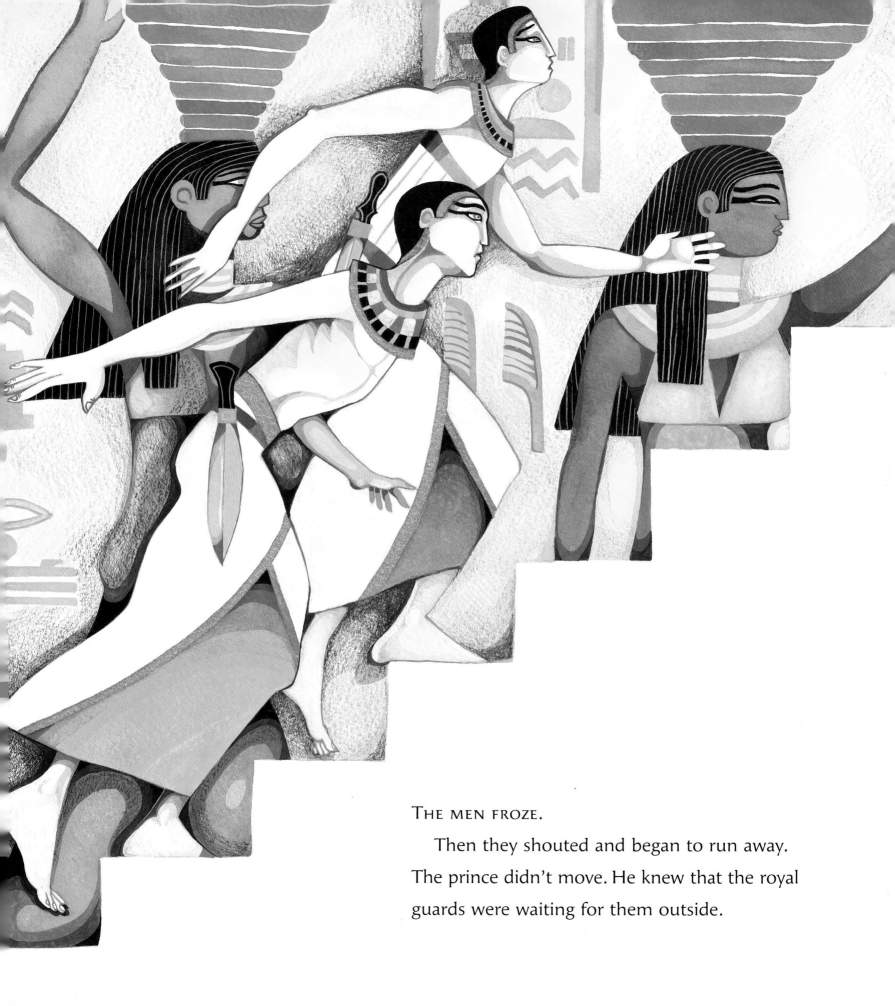

THE MEN FROZE.

Then they shouted and began to run away.
The prince didn't move. He knew that the royal
guards were waiting for them outside.

HE BENT DOWN and gently picked me up.

"As Ra decreed, we meet again," he whispered. "This tomb is no place for you, Khepri. Come, I shall take you back across the river to the temple, where you and I belong."

Now the stars of Egypt burn above me once more.
The night is warm, and my tale is told—a tale that shows
how even a little beetle can play its part in the life of a
great prince.

Historical Background on the Story

MORE THAN five thousand years ago, a great civilization flourished along the banks of the Nile River. Its people were the ancient Egyptians, and still today, the pyramids, temples, and tombs that they built continue to astonish us.

The Egyptians were deeply religious and worshipped many gods. Every animal, tree, and plant held a sacred significance. Their most important god was Ra, the sun god, for the sun brings light to the world—and when it disappears, there is darkness.

In the shadow of night, the Egyptians believed, the sun made a journey through the underworld on a solar boat, to be reborn again the next morning. They gave each stage of the sun's journey a living symbol and chose Khepri, the scarab beetle, to represent the rising sun, portraying him pushing the sun up into the sky.

The Egyptians also believed that their kings, the pharaohs, were the living form of Ra, bestowing life and light on their people as the sun did on the earth. Like the sun, at the end of his life the pharaoh would make a journey through the underworld on a solar boat, to be reborn in the after life.

The pharaoh's body would first be preserved by a process called "mummification" and then placed in his tomb. The early pharaohs built huge pyramids for their resting places, but later kings had underground tombs dug out from solid rock. Here, they stored all the things that they would need for their journey—treasures, weapons, chariots, food, drink, and offerings to the gods.

As soon as his reign began, each pharaoh would begin work on his tomb. The longer he lived, the bigger and better prepared the tomb would be for his death.

But the pharaohs faced a problem: so much treasure all in one place was irresistible to thieves. The kings tried to hide the entrances to their tombs and installed false passages and booby traps, but despite all their efforts, most tombs were eventually found and robbed.

The mysteries of ancient Egypt still intrigue us today. We have managed to unlock some of its secrets, but not all. Who knows how many more lie buried beneath the vast desert sands, still waiting to be discovered?

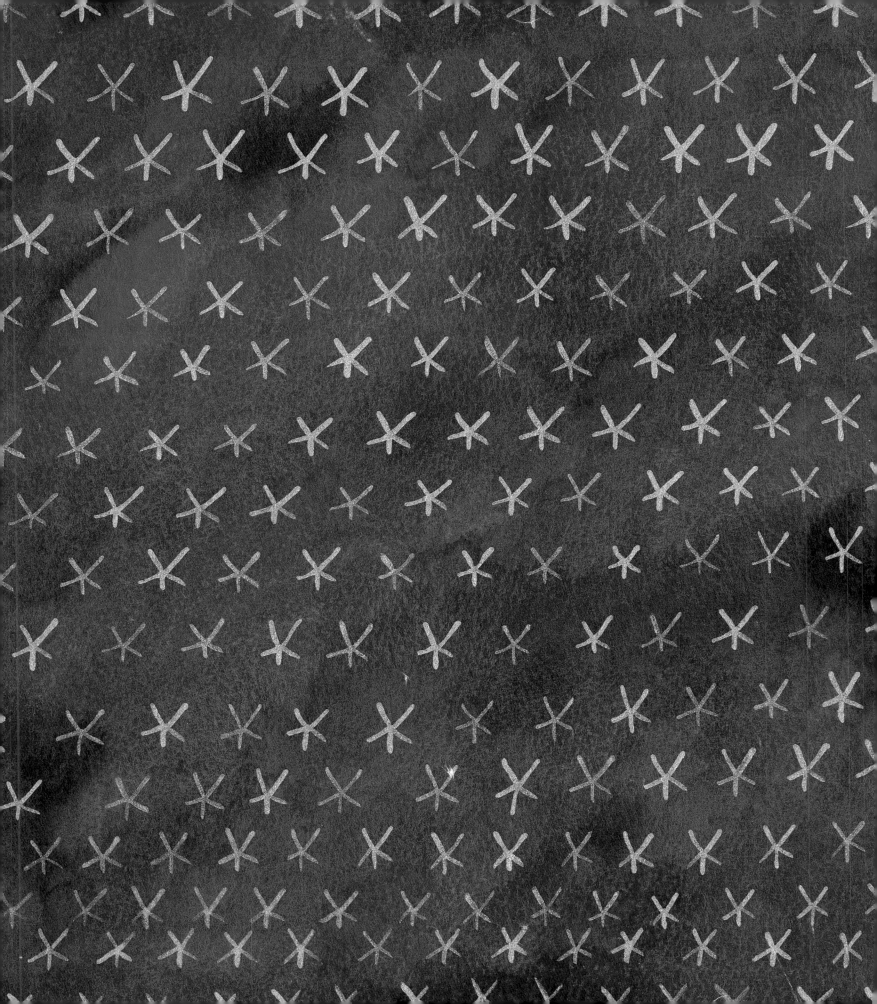